The Berenstain Bears

FORGET THEIR
MANNERS

Etiquette for Bears

"Please" and "Thank you"
Help quite a lot
To make a polite bear
Out of one who is not.

A First Time Book®

The Berenstain Bears
FORGET THEIR MANNERS

Stan & Jan Berenstain

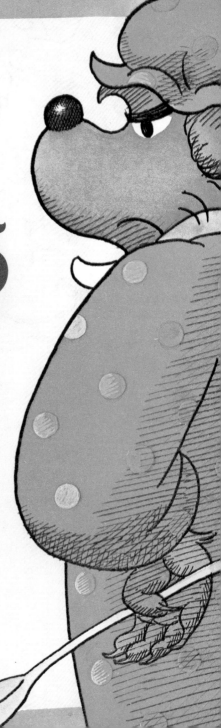

Random House 🏠 New York

Copyright © 1985 by Berenstains, Inc. All rights reserved under International and Pan-American Copyright Conventions. Published in the United States by Random House, Inc., New York, and simultaneously in Canada by Random House of Canada Limited, Toronto.

Library of Congress Cataloging in Publication Data:
Berenstain, Stan. The Berenstain bears forget their manners. SUMMARY: Mama Bear comes up with a plan to correct the Bear family's rude behavior. 1. Children's stories, American. [1. Behavior—Fiction. 2. Bears—Fiction] I. Berenstain, Jan. II. Title. PZ7.B4483Bend 1985 [E] 84-43156 ISBN: 0-394-87333-5 (trade); 0-394-97333-X (lib. bdg.)

Manufactured in the United States of America

77 78 79 80 81 82 83 84 85

There was trouble in the big tree
house down a sunny dirt road deep in
Bear Country—trouble with manners.
The Bear family's trouble with manners
was that they *forgot* them!

At first it was just an occasional "please" or "thank you" that was forgotten.

Then there was a rude push without an "excuse me."

Then a reach across the table instead
of a "please pass the broccoli."

Mama Bear wasn't quite sure how or why it happened. But she was sure of one thing—whatever the reason, the Bear family had become a pushing, shoving, name-calling, ill-mannered mess!

At the table it was even worse. They were a grabbing, mouth-stuffing, food-fighting, kicking-under-the-table super mess!

Of course, Mama Bear tried to correct Brother and Sister Bear's behavior.

She tried coaxing.

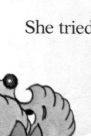

She tried complaining.

She tried shouting!

She tried going to Papa for help (though it sometimes seemed to Mama that he was part of the problem).

Papa banged on the
table and shouted as
only he could shout.
But nothing really
seemed to do any good.

Mama didn't like what was happening to her family. Not one bit. Something had to be done. But what? The best way to fight *bad* habits, she thought, was with *good* habits. Then she thought of a plan. She got a big piece of cardboard and a marker. At the top she wrote:

THE BEAR FAMILY POLITENESS PLAN

When the plan was finished,
she called a family meeting and
showed it to Papa and the cubs.

It certainly got the Bear family's attention!

THE BEAR FAMILY
POLITENESS PLAN

RUDENESS	PENALTY
FORGETTING "PLEASE" OR "THANK YOU" · · ·	SWEEP FRONT STEPS
PUSHING OR SHOVING · · · ·	BEAT 2 RUGS
INTERRUPTING · · ·	DUST DOWNSTAIRS
NAME CALLING · · ·	CLEAN CELLAR
REACHING AT TABLE · · · ·	CLEAN YARD
PLAYING WITH FOOD · · ·	WASH DISHES
RUDE NOISES · · ·	WEED GARDEN
BANGING DOOR · · ·	CLEAN ATTIC
FORGETTING "EXCUSE ME" · · ·	EMPTY GARBAGE
HOGGING BATHROOM · · · ·	PUT OUT TRASH

Mama's plan had a list of all the rude things she wanted to stop. Beside each one was a penalty—a job or chore that went with it. If you forgot a "please" or a "thank you," you had to sweep the front steps. If you pushed or shoved, you had to beat two rugs. If you got caught name calling, you had to clean the whole cellar!

"But, Mama!" sputtered the cubs. "You're not being fair!"

"It seems to me," she said, "that *you're* the ones who aren't being fair—to yourselves or anyone else. That's what manners are all about—being fair and considerate. Manners are very important. They help us get along with each other. Why, without manners—"

"Your mama's absolutely right!" interrupted Papa.

"Thank you, Papa, for your comment. But interrupting is number three on the Rude List, and the penalty is dusting the downstairs," Mama said, and handed him the feather duster.

"Hmm," said Brother. "This looks serious. I think we'd better come up with a plan of our own or we're going to be doing a lot of extra chores."

"What sort of plan?" asked Sister.

"Well," he said, "instead of just being polite, we'll be *super* polite. We'll 'please' and 'thank you' so much that Mama will get fed up and call the whole thing off!"

"Yes," said Sister. "We'll be so polite, she won't be able to stand it!"

They put their plan into action.
They were super polite . . .

—on the stairs:
"After you, Sister dear!"
"Thank you, dear Brother!"

—in the hall:
"Excuse me, Brother
dear!"
"Why, certainly, my
dear Sister!"

—waiting for the bathroom:

"Terribly sorry to have kept you waiting!"

"Think nothing of it, my dear!"

But it didn't work the way they expected. Mama didn't get fed up at all. And after a while Brother and Sister forgot about being super polite and were just polite . . .

—at the table:
   "Pass the honey, please."
   "Certainly."

—in their room:
   "Would you like me to help you pick up your toys?"
   "Thank you very much."

—in the yard:

"Oops! Sorry—I didn't mean to bump you."

"That's all right. No harm done."

And it turned out that Mama had been right: things *did* go more smoothly. Once they got into the good manners habit, they didn't even have to think about it.

But it wasn't so easy for Papa. He was the one who got fed up. It's a little harder to change habits when you're older, and he had to do quite a few extra chores for forgetting his manners.

"I'm glad to get out of the house, away from that Politeness Plan!" he said as he drove the family along the highway on a trip to the supermarket.

"Manners and courtesy are just as important away from home—especially on the road," said Mama as they stopped at a stop sign to let pedestrians and other cars pass. "They help us drive safely."

"Well," grumbled Papa as they all went into the busy supermarket, "I think you can have too much of a good thing— you've got to have common sense along with manners! Why, if you let everyone go ahead of you at the checkout, you'd be there forever!

"And sometimes you *have* to interrupt—
Excuse me, madam," he interrupted a
shopper, "but I believe you have a
leaking bottle in your cart!" The
shopper thanked him for his help.

"You see?" he said, driving home. "There's more to life than remembering your manners. Besides, manners are all right for cubs and mama bears . . .

"...but we papa bears have other things to think about—" At that moment the car in front stopped suddenly and Papa bumped into it. He was furious. "Why, that pinheaded fiddlebrain!" he snarled.

"Name calling!" reminded Sister.

BONK!

The penalty for name calling was cleaning the whole cellar, so Papa gritted his teeth and remembered his manners. And a good thing, too. Because climbing out of the other car was the biggest, angriest bear he had ever seen!

But when the angry bear saw how polite Papa was, he remembered his manners too. He explained that he had stopped short because a mama duck and her ducklings had crossed in front of him. Then he and Papa Bear looked at their bumpers and saw that no harm had been done.

"As I was saying," said Papa as they continued on their way, "it's very important for us to remember our manners at all times—and I want to thank you, Sister, for reminding me to remember mine."

"You're very welcome, I'm sure," said Sister Bear politely.